D1094943

Mousekin's Woodland Sleepers

Mousekin's Woodland Sleepers

story and pictures by
EDNA MILLER

30979

PRENTICE-HALL, Inc.
Englewood Cliffs, N.J.

To Leslie, Jean and Susan

MOUSEKIN'S WOODLAND SLEEPERS
story and pictures by Edna Miller

© 1970 by Edna Miller

Library of Congress Catalog Card Number:
70-107961

ISBN 0-13-604470-0
ISBN 0-13-604561-8 (pbk.)
Printed in the United States of America—J

10   9   8   7   6

Mousekin heard a bird sing
one dark December day.
He peered from beneath his snowy blanket,
half expecting spring . . .
but snow swirled all around him
and through the sleeping woods.
The wind blew hard.
It made the branches sway.

In one large gust
Mousekin found himself sailing
high above the treetops.

When the wind blew downward
he landed in the snow—
bed, blanket and all—
rolling over and over
till he came to a stop
at the foot of an evergreen.
His nest had been a safe warm home
up in the apple tree
with everything a mouse would need
to see a winter through.
Now it lay upon the ground
its lining tossed and scattered.

Mousekin looked all around him.
He knew that he must hide at once
from those who slept as lightly as he
and hunted mice in winter.

He dove beneath the snow
and ran through an icy tunnel.
Mousekin had made many such paths
throughout the winter woods
in case he would have to dash for cover.
He followed this path till he came to the home
of a friendly jumping mouse
far beneath the ground.

Down a narrow passageway
and inside a tiny room
Mousekin found the jumper
curled up in a little ball.
He was fast asleep.

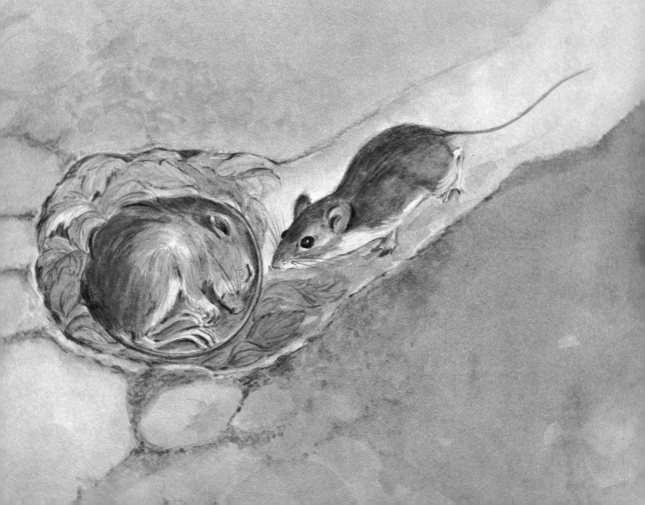

He had seen jumping mice
in the autumn woods
leaping about in search of food . . .
but now the jumper was *very* quiet.
He hardly seemed to breathe.
Mousekin sniffed about the leaf-filled room.
There was no food to be found
and the room was much too small for two.

Mousekin hurried back
to his snow-tunnel up above.
He would have to find a place to live
in the frozen world outside.
Not far from where he peered about
he saw a hollow tree.
When the wind grew still
and all seemed safe
Mousekin raced to the hiding place.

Inside the tree were furry creatures
with leathery wings wrapped close.
They hung by their toes,
head downwards.
Not one made a move.

He had seen these mouse-like creatures
many times before.
They flew about on moonlit nights
trapping insects for their evening meal.
Mousekin nudged one gently
to see if it would move.
But the bat was very *very* still.
It hardly seemed to breathe.
There was no food to be found
in this house either
and nothing with which to build a nest.

Outside the hollow
Mousekin hid in the princess pine
and nibbled wintergreen berries.
Suddenly he spied a dip in the snow cover.
It was a woodchuck's winter home.
Mousekin found the entranceway
underneath the snow.
It was packed tightly with earth and leaves
with just enough room for a mouse to squeeze by.

Mousekin had seen a woodchuck on summer afternoons
sitting in the middle of a large clover bed
as it ate and ate and *ate!*

Now he found the woodchuck asleep
far below the ground.
Many rooms and many tunnels
led to his sleeping chamber.
The woodchuck's paws were tucked beneath him—
his tail wrapped 'round his head.
He was *very* still,
though Mousekin came quite near,
and he scarcely seemed to breathe.

Just as Mousekin curled up to rest
he heard something stir in another room.
In the darkness Mousekin lifted his head
and caught the scent of another creature
he had met in the forest.
The woodchuck had a winter guest,
though he would never know
until he awoke in spring.
Mousekin scrambled through the tunnel
and raced to the opening above.

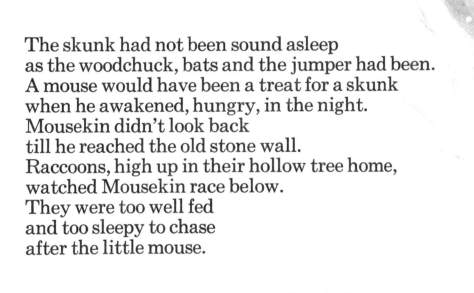

The skunk had not been sound asleep
as the woodchuck, bats and the jumper had been.
A mouse would have been a treat for a skunk
when he awakened, hungry, in the night.
Mousekin didn't look back
till he reached the old stone wall.
Raccoons, high up in their hollow tree home,
watched Mousekin race below.
They were too well fed
and too sleepy to chase
after the little mouse.

Mousekin dove into a chipmunk home
just beneath the cornerstone
of the old rock wall.
He would have much to eat
for he had watched the chipmunk in the fall
making hundreds of trips from the big oak tree,
storing winter food beneath the ground.

The chipmunk slept near the ceiling
on a great pile of acorns and leaves.
He would not be hungry
should he awaken in the night.
Mousekin reached beneath the sleeping form
and took an acorn—quietly.

As soon as Mousekin began to gnaw,
the chipmunk stirred and awoke.
He squeaked sleepily at first,
then squealed angrily at Mousekin
for sampling his winter store.
Mousekin hurried from the burrow—
he wasn't welcome here.

Mousekin ran along the old stone wall
till he came to a cave he had known.
He had explored it many times in summer.
There would be lots of room inside
for a whitefoot mouse to hide.

The entranceway was loosely sealed
with sticks and leaves and stones.
Mousekin searched until he found
a mouse-size opening.
Inside, an enormous creature slept.
His snores filled the cave
with a frightening sound.

Mousekin had seen the bear in early fall
when he stripped great paw-fulls of berries
from branches near the ground.
He had seen him reaching high into trees
for apples, grapes and plums.
Mousekin had not known then
that the bear was fattening for winter.

His large furry body was cozy and warm,
not cold as the jumping mouse
and the woodchuck and the bats had been.
Mousekin ran all around the slumbering bear
to find a place to rest.
When he came to the bear's head,
buried between two giant paws,
the bear moved, opened one eye and growled.
He had not been sound asleep.

Outside the cave, an owl screeched. . . .
Fresh tracks crisscrossed the quiet snow.
Mousekin trembled in the cold
for he knew how dangerous it was
to be a "wide-awake" in winter.

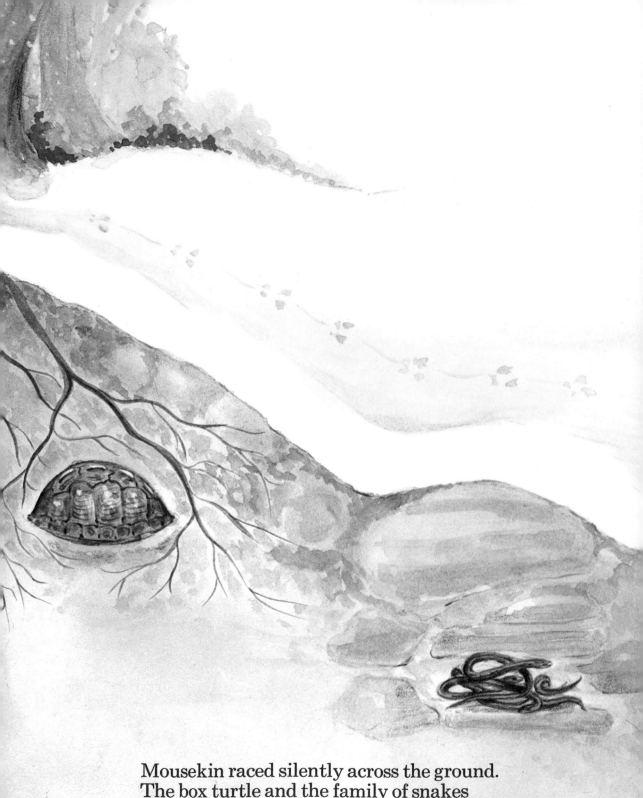

Mousekin raced silently across the ground.
The box turtle and the family of snakes
slept peacefully beneath in their winter homes.

The toad, far below amongst the roots of a tree,
was sleeping deeply too.
Suddenly Mousekin stopped and listened.
He heard something cheering and welcome.
The bird called once again.

The chickadee flew to a feeder—
Mousekin followed him there.
The feeder was filled with millet,
cracked corn and sunflower seeds.
There were bread crumbs and cake crumbs,
bits of apple and raisins,
suet and peanut butter.
Mousekin ate and ate
till he could eat no more.

Night was over and another day had begun.
Mousekin was sleepy now.
On a nearby tree he saw a tiny house.
It was wren-size.
It was mouse-size.
It was just right for a whitefoot mouse.

Mousekin curled up on the bird house floor.
The bedding was soft and warm.
As he closed his eyes in the morning light
he heard happy calls outside.
Some he knew and some were strange—
but all seemed glad and unafraid
to be awake in winter.